MAKING TOY CAR MEMORIES

Written and Illustrated by Duke Yaguchi

Vroom, vroom. Ding, ding. A tanker truck delivered fuel. *Glug, glug, glug.* A tow truck made an emergency call. Mark's shiny, green Ferrari stopped and bought gas.

Mark was Joey's best friend. They played together every day. They especially enjoyed playing with their cars and trucks.

The boys each had a fine collection of toy cars, most of which came in yellow and blue boxes. The various models were pictured on the fronts of the boxes.

The end flaps sported flags of different countries signifying that these toy cars were international. That made them even more special.

Joey pretended that he was actually the driver of each vehicle. His favorite car was the MG 1100 because a dog sat in the back seat, sticking his nose out of the window. He imagined taking "Toby" for a long ride through the mountains. *Arf, arf. Vroom, vroom.*

At the end of each day, Joey carefully returned the cars to their boxes and placed them in a little suitcase.

He was a happy boy with seemingly everything a boy could want—toy cars and a best friend.

But one day, Mark crossed the street to Joey's house without his toy cars. He told Joey that his family would be moving. The friends spent the rest of that day sadly sitting on the front porch. The boys didn't say another word but instead looked at the ground in front of them pressing together to let each other know that they were close by.

Joey was still sitting on the front porch, alone, when his dad came home from work. His dad asked, "How was your day?"

"Awful."

"Why, son?"

"Because Mark's moving away."

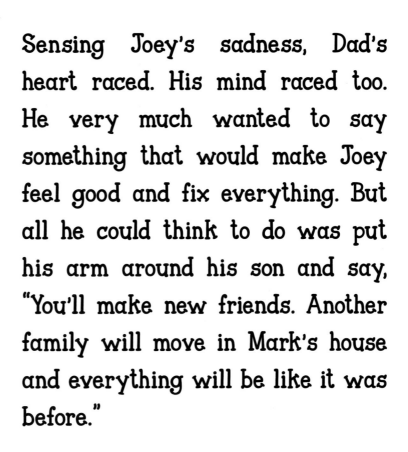

Sensing Joey's sadness, Dad's heart raced. His mind raced too. He very much wanted to say something that would make Joey feel good and fix everything. But all he could think to do was put his arm around his son and say, "You'll make new friends. Another family will move in Mark's house and everything will be like it was before."

Many days passed, and a new family finally did move into Mark's old house. Joey ran over and rang the door bell. *Ding dong.* A young woman holding a girl in her arms opened the door.

#1

"Hi. My name is Joey. I have a toy car here as a present." He peered around the woman, searching for evidence of a boy his age.

"Thank you, Joey. My name is Mrs. Garcia. Would you like to come in?"

Before entering, Joey got down to business. "Do you have children?"

"Yes I do. This is my two-year-old daughter. Her name is Maria."

The lad tried to be more clear, "Do you have anyone my size?"

She shook her head, "No."

"Well, in that case, I'll be going."

"Do you want your car back?"

"No, Maria can keep it. Someday she can build a collection of her own." He turned and sadly walked home.

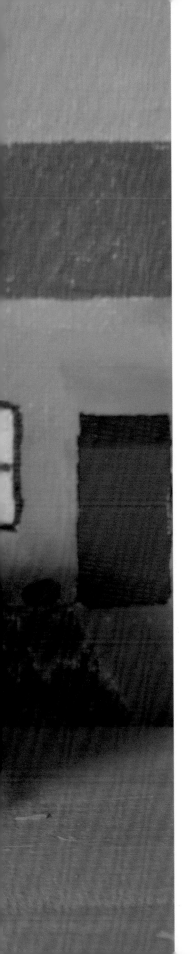

When his dad arrived home from work that day, he noticed a moving van across the street.

"Well son, did you meet our new neighbors? Did you make a new friend?"

Joey told his dad about the family that moved in. His dad could tell that Joey was still sad about his friend moving away. The new neighbors were not going to be able to fill the empty space in Joey's heart left by Mark when he moved away.

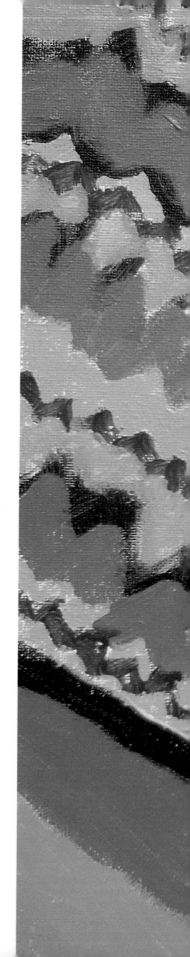

Dad's heart raced. His mind raced too. He very much wanted to say something that would make Joey feel good and fix everything. But all he could think to do was put his arm around his son and say, "You know, even though Mark moved away, he can still be here with you in spirit. You see, you still have those times together when you played, and no one can take those memories away."

"So tomorrow, take out your cars and play like you used to with Mark and enjoy your old toy car memories."

After school, Joey did just that. He carefully took out his cars. A tanker truck delivered fuel. *Glug, glug, glug.* A tow truck made an emergency call with its bright red light flashing. He even pretended Mark was there pumping gas. *Ding, ding.* But Joey had to replace Mark's car with one of his own.

Joey again enjoyed driving his MG with Toby in the back. *Arf, arf, arf.* He drove Toby to a roadside farm stand.

When Joey's father came home, he saw his son sprawled out on the family room floor with his cars. He smiled, sensing that his son had begun to feel better about Mark's absence.

The afternoons repeated like this for an entire week. On Friday, Joey's dad came home and saw his son moping on the family room floor. Although Joey was surrounded by his cars, he wasn't playing.

"What's wrong?" his father asked.

Joey replied, "Well, I like remembering Mark and how we played together. It's like you said, although he's moved away, we still have our memories, and that's good."

"Then I thought, if he hadn't moved, we would have created new memories too. How can I know what I would have missed with Mark?"

Duke Unreality
UNSOLD

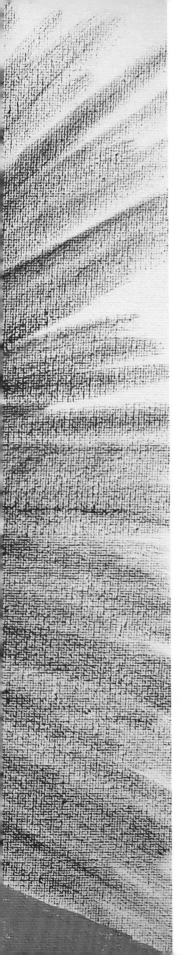

Dad's heart raced. His mind raced too. He so very much wanted to say something that would make Joey feel good and fix everything. But all he could think to do was give his son a big hug and say, "Do you want me to play cars with you?"

Joey looked at his dad and through the tears that had started to form, he smiled and said, "Sure, Dad!" And that's exactly what they did. They started making new toy car memories.

To all of the Joeys out there
and their dads, too.

ACKNOWLEDGEMENTS

Mark Franz, my best friend growing up,
with whom I played cars hundreds of times.

Polly, my wife, editor, and lead cheerleader.

My children Grace, Victor and Rose,
with whom I've loved playing.

Carol Hill, whose photographic talent helped
to showcase my cars.

Matthew and Kyle Syken for posing
as models for some of my paintings.

The Fox Valley Storytelling Guild (Batavia,
Illinois) for their support and encouragement
when I originally created this story.

The Christian Authors Guild (Woodstock,
Georgia) who provided editing suggestions
and lots of encouragement.

Deeds Publishing for helping
make this dream a reality.

About The Author

In sixth grade, when asked, "What do you want to be when you grow up?" Duke answered, "A writer or a comedian."

After spending nearly 33 years with IBM, Duke is finally fulfilling his dream first spoken in that classroom in 1967.

Duke began painting in 2010. Most of his works are modern art. "This way," he says wryly, "no one can know if I made a mistake." The reason he began painting was to create decor for his home. As he puts it, "It's the only way we can afford original art!"

He currently blogs Daily Devotions twice a month for the Pilgrimage United Church of Christ in Marietta, Georgia. He is working on a major book intended to inspire divorcing men to reconnect with their children, their God as well as themselves.

Duke resides in Marietta with his wife, Polly, and their dogs Hachi, Toby, and Nicole. You can write Duke at dukeyaguchi@gmail.com or visit with him at dukeyaguchi.com.

Printed in the United States of America

Published by Deeds Publishing, Marietta, GA
www.deedspublishing.com

Library of Congress Cataloging-in-Publications Data is available on request.

ISBN 978-1-941165-60-7

Books are available in quantity for promotional or premium use. For information, write Deeds Publishing, PO Box 682212, Marietta, GA 30068 or info@deedspublishing.com.

First edition, 2015

10 9 8 7 6 5 4 3 2 1